WRITTEN BY

Julia Donaldson

ILLUSTRATED BY

David Roberts

The Troll

MACMILLAN
CHILLDREN'S BOOKS

For Lisa – J.D.

For Cushion – D.R.

First published 2009 by Macmillan Children's Books
a division of Macmillan Publishers Limited
20 New Wharf Road, London N1 9RR

Basingstoke and Oxford

Associated companies throughout the world

www.panmacmillan.com

ISBN: 978-0-230-01793-1

Text copyright © Julia Donaldson 2009
Illustrations copyright © David Roberts 2009

Moral rights asserted. All rights reserved. No part of this publication may be reproduced, stored in or introduced into a retrieval system, or transmitted, in any form, or by any means (electronic, mechanical, photocopying, recording or otherwise), without the prior written permission of the publisher.

Any person who does any unauthorized act in relation to this publication may be liable to criminal prosecution and civil claims for damages.

A CIP catalogue record for this book is available from the British Library.

Printed in Belgium by Proost   9 8 7 6 5 4 3 2 1

There was once a troll who lived under a bridge. (That's where trolls are supposed to live.)

Meanwhile, far out at sea,
there were some pirates
who lived in a ship.
(That's where pirates are
supposed to live.)

Trolls are supposed to eat goats,
but no goats ever came trip-trapping
over this troll's little bridge.
So he ate fish instead.

But one morning he heard a faint
noise on his bridge. Up he popped,
and he said what trolls are supposed
to say, which is . . .

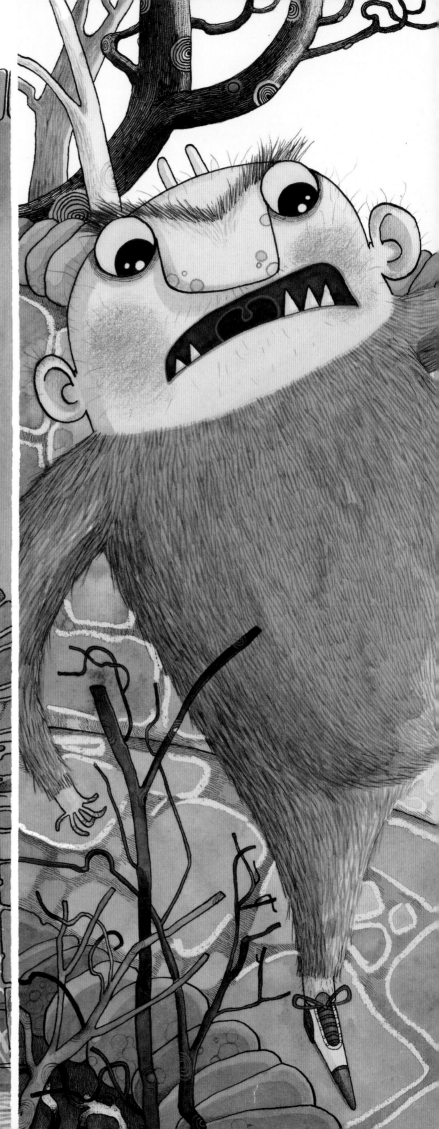

"WHO'S THAT TRIP-TRAPPING OVER MY BRIDGE?"

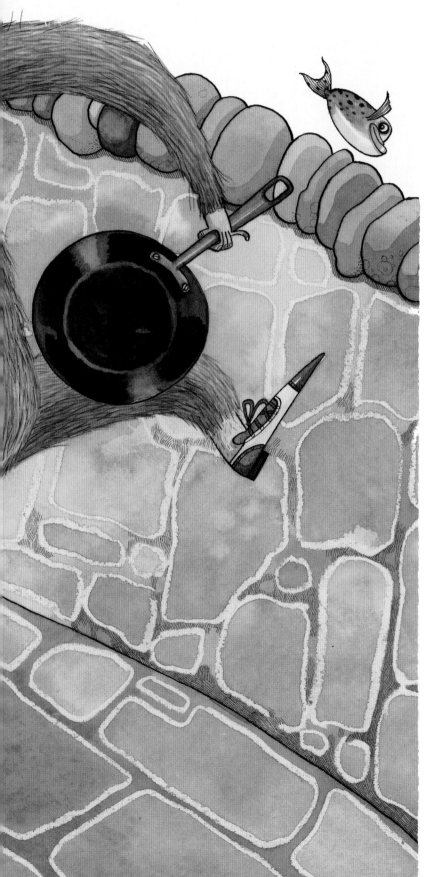

"I'm not trip-trapping, I'm scuttling," said a tiny black creature. "And I'm a spider."

"Oh bother, I thought you were a goat," said the troll.

"No – goats have fur," said the spider.

"Never mind, I'll eat you anyway," said the troll. "You'll make a nice change from fish."

"Oh please don't eat me!" said the spider. "Why don't you go further down the river to the next bridge? It's a much better bridge for goats."

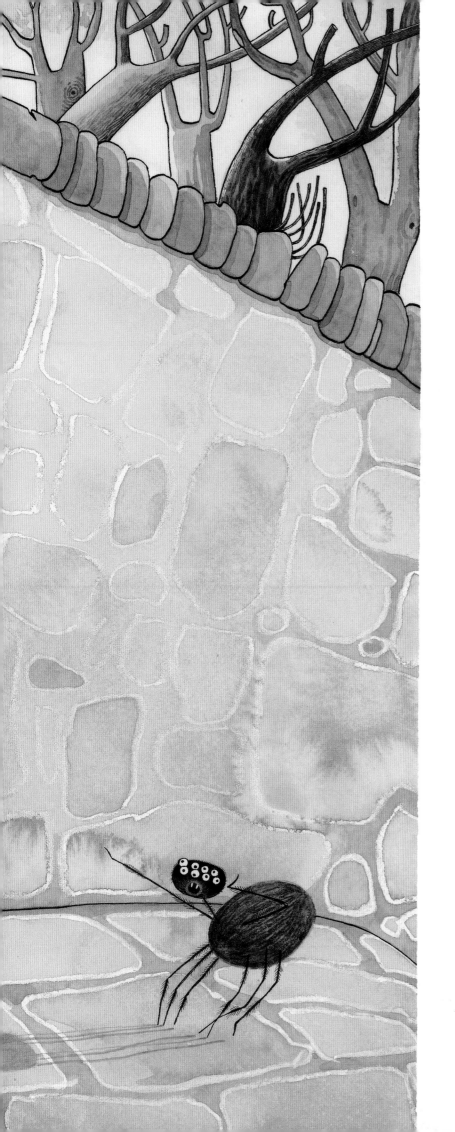

"All right then," said the troll.
So he packed up his frying pan and
his cookery book, and off he strode.

Pirates are supposed to dig for treasure, and these pirates had a treasure map with a rhyme on it.

Between the palm tree and the rocks,
Six foot deep lies a treasure box.

They sailed and they sailed until they reached an island.

"This is the spot," said Hank Chief. "Start digging!"

The pirates dug and they dug, but all that they found was a grumpy mole.

"It must be the wrong island," they said.

All that digging had made them hungry.

It was Ben Buckle's turn to do the cooking. He cooked fish pie.

"It's soggy," said Percy Patch.

"It's slimy," said Peg Polkadot.

"When we find the gold we can buy a decent cookery book," said Hank Chief.

And they set sail again.

The troll was sitting under his new, middling-sized bridge, reading his cookery book. Suddenly he heard a sound above his head. Up he popped.

"WHO'S THAT TRIP-TRAPPING OVER **MY BRIDGE?**" he roared.

"I'm not trip-trapping,
I'm pattering," said
a furry creature.
"And I'm a mouse."

"Oh bother, I thought you were
a goat," said the troll.

"No — goats have longer ears,"
said the mouse.

"Never mind, I'll eat you anyway," said
the troll. "I'm getting sick of fish."

"Oh please don't eat me," said the
mouse. "Why don't you go down
to the next bridge? There are goats
trip-trapping over that one all the time."

"Very well," said the troll, and
he packed up his things again
and off he strode.

Meanwhile the pirates had discovered another island.

They dug and they dug, but all that they found was a rusty old bucket with a crab in it.

"It's the wrong island again," they said.

That night Percy Patch did the cooking. He cooked fish soup.

"It's bony," said Ben Buckle.

"It's briny," said Peg Polkadot.

"If only we could find the gold, we could pay
for a proper cook," said Hank Chief.

The troll was frying fish under his new, big bridge when he heard a sound above his head. Up he popped.

"WHO'S THAT TRIP-TRAPPING OVER MY BRIDGE?" he bellowed.

"I'm not trip-trapping, I'm lolloping,"
said a creature with long ears.
"And I'm a rabbit."

"Oh bother, I thought you were
a goat," said the troll.

"No – goats have hoofs," said the rabbit.

"Never mind, I'll eat you anyway," said
the troll. "Anything's better than fish."

"Oh please don't eat me," said the
rabbit. "Why don't you walk down
to the next bridge? There are herds of
goats trip-trapping over that one."

"Are you sure?" asked the troll.
Once again he packed up, and
off he strode.

Meanwhile the pirates were digging on a new island.
They dug and they dug, but all that they found was an old
wellington boot with a nest of centipedes in it.

"We'll never find the right island," they said.

That night it was Peg Polkadot's turn to do the cooking. She cooked fishcakes.

"They're sticky," said Ben Buckle.

"They're sandy," said Percy Patch.

Hank Chief said nothing.
He was too busy being sick over the side of the ship.

The troll's river grew wider and wider.
Then it stopped being a river and it flowed into the sea.
The troll found himself on a sandy beach.

"There isn't another bridge," he said.
"That rabbit was tricking me."
But then he spotted some hoof prints in the sand.

"A goat at last!" he cried. He looked around, but he
couldn't see any goats. "Never mind – it will probably
come back tomorrow," he said.
The troll followed the hoof prints . . .

They led him to a spot between a tall palm tree and two big rocks.

"I know!" he thought. "I'll dig a pit. Then tomorrow the goat will fall into it and I can eat it."

The troll dug and dug with his
frying pan. Just when he thought
the hole was deep enough the
pan hit something hard.
It was a great big chest.

"Perfect," said the troll. "I can
hide in here and keep warm. Then
when the goat falls into the hole
I'll open the lid and pop up."

He lifted the lid. The chest was
full of round gold things.

"These are no use to me," he said, and he threw them all into the sea. Then he climbed into the chest and lay down.

"Tomorrow I can have goat for breakfast instead of fish!" he thought as he drifted off to sleep.

It was dark when the pirates arrived
at the next island.
"This is the spot," said Hank Chief.

"But someone's been digging here
already!" said Ben Buckle.

"Don't say they've found the treasure
before us!" said Percy Patch.

"No, look! Here it is!" cried Peg Polkadot.
The chest was heavy.
"It must be full of gold!" said Hank Chief. "Quick!
Back to the ship before anyone stops us."

The troll was woken by a loud bang.

"That's my breakfast falling into the hole!" he thought.

But why was the chest heaving and swaying? And why was the lid opening? Surely goats couldn't open lids?

The lid opened wide. Staring down at the troll were four angry pirates.

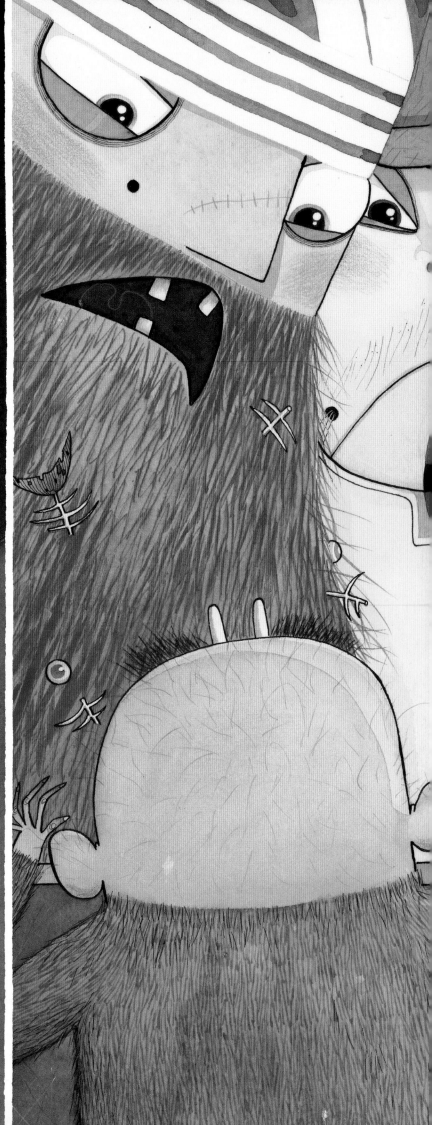

"Where's the gold?" shouted Hank Chief.

"I – I – threw it into the sea," said the troll.

"The plank! The plank!" yelled Ben Buckle and Percy Patch. "Make him walk the plank!"

The next second, the pirates were pushing him on to it.

"WHO'S THAT TRIP-TRAPPING

OVER MY PLANK?" jeered Hank Chief.

"I'm not trip-trapping, I'm shuffling,"
said the troll in a very small voice.
"And I'm a troll."

He reached the end of the plank.
His knees were knocking.

"JUMP!"

yelled the pirates.

But just then, Peg Polkadot came running up.

"Wait!" she cried. "I've found something else inside the chest!" In one hand she held the troll's frying pan. In the other hand she held his cookery book.

"Stop!"

called Hank Chief.

He looked at the troll in a new way. "Can you cook?" he asked. "Yes," said the troll and "YES!" shouted the pirates.

"Then you can stay," said Hank Chief.

"Thank you!" said the troll, and he shuffled back along the plank. "When shall I start?"

"Now," said Hank.

The pirates showed the troll the ship's kitchen. The troll grinned. He turned to his favourite page in his cookery book.

"Shall I make us a nice goat stew?" he asked.

"Goat? GOAT? But pirates don't eat goat!" said Hank Chief. "We want what pirates are supposed to eat."

"And what's that?" asked the troll.

"Fish,"

said the pirate chief.